The Day the Leader Was Killed

NAGUIB MAHFOUZ

Translated by Malak Mashem

ANCHOR BOOKS

A DIVISION OF RANDOM HOUSE, INC.

NEW YORK

AN ANCHOR ORIGINAL, JUNE 2000

Library of Congress Cataloging-in-Publication Data
Mahfuz, Najib, 1911–
[Yawma qutila al-za'im. English]
The day the leader was killed / Naguib Mahfouz ; translated
by Malak Hashem.
p. cm.
ISBN 0-385-49922-1 (trade pbk.)
I. Hashem, Malak.   II. Title
PJ7846.A46 Y3813 2000
892.7'36—dc21   00-024572

Book design by Oksana Kushnir

www.anchorbooks.com

Printed in the United States of America
10 9 8 7 6 5 4 3 2

NAGUIB MAHFOUZ

The Day the Leader Was Killed

Naguib Mahfouz is the most prominent author of
Arabic fiction published in English today. He was
born in Cairo in 1911 and began writing when he
was seventeen. A student of philosophy and an
avid reader, he has been influenced by many West-
ern writers, including Flaubert, Balzac, Zola,
Camus, Tolstoy, Dostoevsky, and, above all,
Proust. He has more than thirty novels to his credit,
ranging from his earliest historical romances to his
most recent experimental novels. In 1988, Mr.
Mahfouz was awarded the Nobel Prize in Litera-
ture. He lives in the Cairo suburb of Agouza with
his wife and two daughters.

THE FOLLOWING TITLES BY NAGUIB MAHFOUZ ARE
ALSO PUBLISHED BY ANCHOR BOOKS:

The Thief and the Dogs

The Beginning and the End

Wedding Song

The Beggar

Respected Sir

Autumn Quail

The Time and the Place and other stories

The Search

Midaq Alley

The Journey of Ibn Fattouma

Miramar

Adrift on the Nile

The Harafish

Arabian Nights and Days

Children of the Alley

Echoes of an Autobiography

Akhenaten

The Cairo Trilogy:
Palace Walk
Palace of Desire
Sugar Street

The Day the Leader Was Killed

The Day the Leader Was Killed

Muhtashimi Zayed

Little sleep. Then a moment of expectation full of warmth beneath the heavy cover. The window lets in a faint streak of light which powerfully penetrates the forbidding darkness of the room. O Lord, I sleep at Thy command and awaken at Thy command! Thou art Lord of things. There goes the call to the dawn prayer marking the birth of a new day for me. There it is calling Thy name from the depth of silence. O Lord, help me tear myself away from my warm bed and face the bitter cold of this long winter! My dear one is bundled up deep in sleep in the other bed. Let me grope my way in the dark so as not to wake him up. How cold the ablution water is! But I derive warmth from Thy mercy. Prayer is communion and annihilation. God loves those who love to commune with Him. Blessed not is the day in which I draw not closer to the Lord.

At long last, I tear myself away from my reveries to

awaken those asleep. I am the alarm clock of this exhausted household. It is good to be of some use at this advanced age of mine. Old, indeed, but healthy, praised be the Lord! Now it is all right to switch on the light and knock on the door, calling, "Fawwaz," till I am able to hear his voice crying out, "Good morning, Father."

I then return to my room and switch on the light there too. Here lies my grandson, fast asleep, nothing showing except the center of his face, tucked in between bedcover and bonnet. Nothing doing. I must drag him out of the realm of peace and into hell.

My heart goes out to him and his generation as I whisper, "Elwan, wake up." He opens his light brown eyes and yawns as he mutters with a smile, "Good morning, Grandpa."

This is followed by a rush of feet and a loosening of tongues as life begins to throb between the bathroom and the dining room. I sit and listen to the morning recitation of the Quran on the radio until Hanaa, my daughter-in-law, cries out, "Uncle, breakfast is ready!" Food is the single most important thing that remains for me out of the pleasures of life. Manifold indeed are God's blessings in this life of ours. O Lord, protect me from sickness and disability. No one any longer to take care of anyone anymore. And no money left over in case of sickness. Woe unto him who falls! Now it is beans or falafel for breakfast. Both of these are more impor- tant than the Suez Canal. Gone are the days of eggs, cheese, pastrami, and jam. Those were the days of the an- cien régime or B.I.—that is, Before *Infitah,* Sadat's open-door economic policy. Prices have long since rocketed; everything has gone berserk. On a diet rich in bread, Fawwaz continues to gain weight. Hanaa too, but she is also aging prematurely. At fifty, today, one appears to be sixty.

"On certain days now, we'll have to be working mornings and evenings at the Ministry, so I'll have to give up my job at the firm," said Fawwaz in his loud voice.

I grew perturbed. Both he and his wife work in a private-sector firm. Their income, my pension, and Elwan's salary combined are hardly sufficient to meet the bare necessities of life, so how would it be if he were to leave the firm?

"It may be for just a short while," I said in a hopeful tone.

"I'll do some of your work for you and bring the rest home. And I'll explain your circumstances to the Chief of Division," said Hanaa.

"That means I'd have to work from crack of dawn to midnight," Fawwaz retorted angrily.

I have always been hoping that we could try not to discuss our problems at mealtimes. But how?

"The father of my professor, Alyaa Samih, drives a cab in his spare time and, of course, earns much more this way," said Elwan.

"Does he own the cab?" his father asked him.

"I think so."

"And how would I buy one? Is your professor's father rich or does he take bribes?"

"All I know is that he's a respectable man."

"When all's said and done, he has chosen a respectable path," I said.

"Maybe one day I'll choose a similar path," Elwan said, laughing.

"What would you do?" asked Hanaa in all earnestness.

"I'd round up a gang to rob banks!"

"Best thing you can do," snapped back Fawwaz.

I wiped the dishes properly and Hanaa took them back to the kitchen. The moment they had said goodbye and left, I found myself, as usual, all alone in the small flat. O Lord, provide for them and protect them from the vicissitudes of time! O Lord, grant me the grace of Thy protection! Were I to leave this house as it is, it would remain a total mess until the evening. I do what I can with my bedroom and the living room, where I while away my solitude listening to the Quran, to songs, and to the news on the radio and television. Had there been a fourth room, Elwan could have settled down in it. Praised be the Lord, I do not question His authority.

One day, Abu al-Abbas al-Mursi, the pious sage, came across a group of people crowding around a bakery in Cairo in a year when prices had risen tremendously. His heart went out to them. It occurred to him that if he had had some small change, he could have helped these people, whereupon he felt some weight in his pocket. When he put his hand in it, he found a few coins, which he promptly gave to the baker in exchange for some bread, which he went on to dole out to the people. After he had left, the baker discovered that the coins were false. So he cried out for help until he caught the man, who then realized that the feelings of pity he had felt for the people had been a sort of objection on his part to God's ways to men. Repentant, he begged the Lord's forgiveness and, no sooner had he done that, than the baker realized that the coins had in fact been genuine! That is indeed a perfectly holy man. Holiness is bestowed only upon those who shun the world. I am close to eighty but am unable to shun the world. It is God's world and His short-lasting gift to us, so how am I to shun it? I love it, but with the love of one who is a free, devout worshiper. Why, then, doest Thou begrudge me holiness?

I am interested in the Quran and the Hadith, just as I am interested in the *Infitah* and in my beans mixed with oil, cumin, and lemon. When will I be graced with God's boundless mercy so that I may one day be able to point to the light from afar and it would just be switched on without my ever having to touch the light switch? I have only one good friend left and, even then, old age has come between us. Solitude of the soul, of place, and of time. It is a year now since I was last able to read. I get very little sleep, but I am not afraid of death. I shall welcome it when it comes, but not before it is due.

When King Fuad inaugurated our school, I was called upon to give a speech on behalf of the teachers. A day of glory. My heart warmed as the pupils cheered: "Long live the King, long live Saad Zaghloul!" The cheering has changed and so have the songs. Prices have exploded. Behind the closed panes, I can see the River Nile and the trees. Our house is the oldest and smallest one on Nile

Street: a dwarf amid modern buildings. The River Nile itself has changed and, like me, it is struggling against loneliness and old age. We share the same predicament: it, too, has lost its glory and grandeur and is now no longer even able to get into a tantrum. And then, so much poverty and so many loved ones departed; so many cars, so many fortunes! A cloudy day with premonitions of rain. On such days, it was fun to go on a trip to the Qanater Gardens. Old friends would get together for a meal of fried chicken, potatoes, and drinks. And the record player playing old favorites. They are all skeletons now and their carefree, mirthful laughter has gone with the wind! They all stood behind me in a row on my wedding night, the night I unveiled Fatma for the first time. Five years have gone by since I last visited your grave. What mad speed and what crowds, the likes of which the trees have never witnessed since they were planted in the days of Khedive Ismail! Madmen rush unawares to meet their fate in accidents. The Prophet, God bless him and grant him salvation, said: "Ye slave of God, be in this world as a stranger or passerby and reckon yourself among the dead." The Messenger of God has truly spoken.

Elwan Fawwaz Muhtashimi

The beginning of a new day. Old. New, old. New, old. New, old. New, old. Old, new. Dizzying. If there can't be old that is good, then let there be new that is bad. Anything is better than nothing. Death itself is novelty. Walking is health and a means of economizing. It's supposed to be the road to love and beauty and look what it is! Ouch, my feet! Ouch, my shoes! Endure and be patient, for this is the age of endurance and having to be patient. In these days of fire and brutes, no breeze to cool the heart but you, my love. Still one must be grateful to the majestic trees and, above all, to the River Nile. Look up above, at the white clouds and the treetops so that you may forget the pockmarked surface of the earth. One day, you'll meet an innocent devil and befriend him. I bow to the all-powerful mind, to nobility of character and to profound thought.

I have lived in this old house, lost amid towering

buildings—an intruder among the rich—since child-hood through adolescence and young adulthood. One of these days, the landlord will kill us. Amazing that love should survive amid this ever-spreading corruption. Is this shaky sidewalk the remnant of an air raid? Rubbish heaps lying there in corners guarding lovers. Good morning, you people, piled up in buses, your faces looking out behind cracked glass panes like those of prisoners on visiting days. And the bridge bursting with passersby. Cyclists greedily—but unremittingly—devouring bean sandwiches.

"With every mounting crisis comes relief," said my grandfather.

Dear Grandpa, till when will we go on learning things off by heart and parroting others? He's my best friend. And I'm but an orphan. I lost my parents when they lost themselves in continuous work from morning to night, shuttling between the government and private sector to eke out a meager living. We meet only fleetingly.

"No time for idle philosophizing, please. Can't you see that we can't even find time for sleep?"

When any of my sisters quarrel with their husbands, I'm the one who's sent over to try to patch things up! These days, no one finds anyone to help. We all have to struggle, and finally it's you and your luck! Here now is that food company—one of the public-sector firms—on the entrance of which you can read in bold print: ENTER HERE WITHOUT HOPE. And, finally, there is my sweet-heart seated in our office: Public Relations and Transla-tion. She looks at me with a smile suffused with love.

"Had you waited a few minutes, we would've come together," I reprimanded her.

"For reasons I won't bother you with, I had to have breakfast at the Brazilian Coffee Stores Café," she answered cheerfully.

Thanks to my grandfather, we were able to be in the same company and in the selfsame division. Rather, it was thanks to one of the Free Officers who had, at one time, been one of his pupils. My grandfather is an unforgettable character so that even those who would normally not acknowledge the good offices of their predecessors would nevertheless have to acknowledge their debt to my grandfather. There are so many women in our division. Piles of paper crowding our work, paperwork that needs no serious effort of concentration. I work a little and then steal a glance at Randa.

I reminisce and dream. I dream and reminisce. A long story going back to the beginning of time in our old house, the only one of its kind. We played together as children. We were the same age. Mama insists—she has no proof—that she is older than I. Puberty comes along and, with it, a certain bashfulness and wariness. My conscience pricks me, dampening all pleasures. But ultimately love got the upper hand. It was during our secondary-school days. On the staircase, midway between both landings, we would indulge in fleeting flirtations and insinuations. One day, I flung a letter of confessions into her hands. In reply, she offered me a novel entitled *The Loyalty of Two Generations*. When, in the same year, we both passed our secondary-school examinations, I told my grandfather that I wanted to get engaged to our neighbor, Randa Sulayman.

My grandfather told me that, in his day, one was not allowed to talk about an engagement before one became totally independent. But he promised he would open up the subject with Father and Mother. He also promised to give me a hand. My mother said that the family of Sulayman Mubarak was closer to us than our own relatives, and that Randa was just like one of her daughters. "But she is older than you!" My father said, "She's your age if not a little older and just as poor!"

Our engagement was announced on a happy day. In those days, a dream could still come true. But the moment we started working we had to face a new set of problems. Three years went by, and we turned twenty-six. I was in love then, but now I am exhausted, helpless, and burdened with responsibilities. We no longer meet just to talk but to engage in endless discussions, enough to allow us to qualify for the Economics Group: the flat, the furniture, the burdens of a life together. Neither she nor I have a solution. We have only love and determination. Our engagement was announced in the Nasser era and we were made to face reality in the days of *Infitah*. We sank in the whirlpool of a mad world. We are not even eligible for emigration. There is no demand for philosophy or history majors. We are redundant. So many redundant people. How did we get to this point of no return? I am a man persecuted and burdened with responsibilities and doubts; she is pretty and desirable. There I stand, broad as a dam, blocking her path.

Everywhere I see her parents' angry looks. I can

almost hear what is being said behind my back. And over and above that float the dreams of reform. They come from above or from below through resolutions or revolutions! The miracle of science and production! But what of what is being said about corruption and crooks? What Alyaa Samih and Mahmud al-Mahruqi are saying is just awful. What is right? Why have I become suspicious of everything since the fall of my idol in June 1967? How do people find a magic formula for amassing colossal wealth in record time? Could this happen without corruption? What is the secret of my insistence on remaining a man of principles? All I aspire to at this point is to be able to marry Randa.

Randa and I have been asked to meet Anwar Allam, the Chief of Division. We are summoned together since we work together on translating the statutes. He's a pleasant, gregarious sort of man and loves to show off: slim, tall, and dark, with round eyes and a sharp look. He's also an old man approaching his fifties and a bachelor.

"Hello, my bride- and bridegroom-to-be!" said Anwar Allam in his usual manner.

He started looking at our work, hurriedly but intelligently making some remarks here and there. As he returned the draft, he inquired, "When is the happy day?"

Although I imagine that it is his policy to interfere in the private lives of the employees, I am not comfortable about it, just as I am not comfortable about the look in his eyes. I do like him, though.

"We have, until now, found no solution to our problem."

"No problem without a solution," he said with bold contempt.

"But . . ." I said as one on the point of objecting.

"Don't keep repeating what all helpless people say," he said, interrupting me suddenly.

"What do you think is the solution?" I asked, much annoyed.

"Don't turn to others for solutions," he said, laughing in an irritating way.

I returned to my desk with one idea haunting me: he had deliberately tried to depict me as an utterly helpless person in Randa's presence. I was obsessed with this idea the whole while until it was time to leave. As we returned together to Nile Street, wrapped up in our coats, I told her:

"The man got on my nerves."

"Mine too," she said, pulling up the collar of her coat securely around her lovely neck.

"He's revolting and thinks he's smart."

"That's right."

"Do you believe there's a solution to our problem that hasn't occurred to us yet?"

She mused a little and then said:

"I have great faith in God, yet we keep believing that everything will remain the same forever."

"But time is flying, Randa," I said, perturbed.

"Maybe, but love is constant!" she said, smiling.

Randa Sulayman Mubarak

I climb the stairs to the apartment while he stands in front of his flat as if to make sure that I have reached my door safely. He said good-bye with a lukewarm kiss like one worried, wrapped up in his own thoughts. Damn the boss! He irritated him for no good reason. And, all the while, he remained depressed and downcast. I can understand this well, but, then, doesn't he trust me? There's no room for further anxiety. The smell of *mulukhiya* soup is floating about in the apartment. It really whets my appetite.

Is Father asleep on the sofa? His head is drooping slowly but surely. He smiles affectionately. You have grown weaker and frailer. Damn that rheumatism! Muhtashimi Bey, my darling one's grandfather, is ten years older but ten times stronger. Mama's voice announces that lunch is ready. I like *mulukhiya* soup. Mama, though, doesn't think much of my appetite.

"When one is thin, one cannot fight off diseases," she often tells me.

"Obesity is just as hazardous," I answer her.

"Stubborn . . . if I say aye, she says nay."

Mama is obese and has always been so. She prays seated on the sofa. Just because of that, I'm careful about what I eat. She thinks she is well-off just because she has an income of twenty-five pounds a month. She may have been right as far as those legendary days she tells us about go. But, nowadays, how much are her income, Papa's pension, and my salary combined worth?!

Papa has just inserted his dental apparatus which he uses only when he eats. He starts to eat slowly, complaining of the bitter cold. Sanaa, my sister—a divorcee who shares my room—has come to join us too. She's taking secretarial courses in a private institute in the hope of finding a job. She doesn't want to be a burden on anyone. After lunch, I lay on my bed and again recalled the lukewarm kiss. I don't like this. It's an insult or almost so. If this is repeated, I'll tell him frankly not to kiss me unless he really feels like it and when he isn't preoccupied with anything other than his love for me. What remains now but love? I take care of him as though I'm his mother and he's a spoiled, rebellious child. Oh, if only he could have been an engineer! He would probably have been among the heroes of the *Infitah* rather than one of its victims. He's also a victim of June 1967 and the disappearance of the vanquished hero. He's confused and uncommitted. But for how much longer will this go on? He's contemptuous of those who have preceded him and believes he's better than the whole lot of them. Why? When will he start looking at himself critically and objectively?

Maybe this is my job, my role, but then—again—I'm worried about the only thing that remains: our love. I love him and love is irrational. I want him, heart and soul. How? When? My sister Sanaa made a love match, was content with her secondary-school certificate, with being a housewife, and having a landed young gentleman for a husband. But it didn't work out and love simply died. As usual, accusing fingers were pointed at the other party. But she's a nervous person and erupts like a volcano for the most trivial reasons. Who can tolerate that?! It's for this reason that I try not to fly into a temper much the same way as I'm careful about what I eat. When will that damned happiness be possible? How long can beauty hold out against the whips and lashes of time?

No, I only know I had fallen asleep because of the dream I had. It was afternoon when I woke up. I cuddled my cat for a moment, then I performed the noon and afternoon prayers at one go. I have Mama to thank, for she has been my religious mentor. As for Papa, Mama is happy with her lot though, despite the age difference between them, and in spite of Papa's atheism! Do you remember how you used to reproach him in the early days?

"Papa, why don't you fast like the rest of us?"

"The little one is reproaching her father," he would say as he laughed.

"Don't you fear God?"

"Health, my dear. Don't be misled by appearances."

"And prayers, Papa?"

"Oh! I'll talk to you about that when you grow older."

That's not how things are at my sweetheart's. His grandfather, father, and mother pray and fast. My father's atheism is as obvious today as the fact that he is old and in poor health. He has never uttered a skeptical word but his behavior is proof enough. In his fits of anger, he curses religion. He may have repented and asked God's forgiveness for my sake or for Mother's, but it's no more than a slogan like the rest of those hollow slogans that the authorities hurl at us. A nauseating age of slogans! Even the late hero never tired of reiterating slogans. Between the slogans and the truth is an abyss in which we have all fallen and lost ourselves. But how about my sweetheart? Religious? Nonreligious? Committed? Uncommitted? Alyaa Samih? Mahmoud al-Mahruqi? Oh! he's my sweetheart and that's enough. The rest is me and my luck! He's forever in quest of something lost. Had there been a solution to our problem, he would have been able to take it easy and rest. Meanwhile, he hurls himself against rocks and clutches at thin air.

Here we are, all together in the living room: my father with his poor health, his problems of old age, and his atheistic ways; Mama with her excessive obesity and the worries of others; Sanaa with her dissatisfaction with her lot and her painful feeling of alienation; and me and my chronic problem. On the face of it, my parents have accomplished their mission, but how ironical! Here I am, again besieged by that silent inquisition. What then after an engagement that has lasted eleven years? Is there no glimmer of hope?

"Let her go on waiting until she's widowed and still only engaged," says Sanaa in her shrill voice.

"It's nothing to do with you," I tell her firmly.

"Randa, keep reminding him or else he'll forget," Mama says.

"We're living with our worries day in, day out, so there's no point in reminding him." And then, more sharply: "I am of age and have made my choice of my own free will, and I will not regret anything."

"Randa is old enough and can take care of herself," says my father, annoyed.

"We've lost so many good opportunities," Mama says with regret.

"I'm not a slave girl on sale at the market!" I retort in a proud tone.

"I am your mother, and irreproachable. I got married in the old-fashioned way and have, thank God, made a good match."

"Look, Mama, every generation has its own style, but ours has been by far the unluckiest of them all."

"There was a time when people ate dogs, donkeys, and children. Then people started eating each other!" says my father with a smile.

"Let's hope we'll fare better than that age of cannibalism," I retorted bitterly.

"For heaven's sake, the TV series has started," my father cried out in an attempt to change the subject.

The theme tune of which I am so fond wafted me out of my conflict. Thanks to its magical power, I was able to conjure up my sweetheart who seemed to drop out of the blue and seat himself beside me. I was suddenly transformed into a dreamy-eyed woman with a profound understanding of married life. I fought back a treacherous tear which was on the verge of disgracing me. Is life possible without him?

"The heroes of TV series are really lucky! They find the solution to their problems in no time!" said Mama.

Muhtashimi Zayed

In my solitude, I wait. I tighten the robe around my frail body and rearrange the bonnet on my bald head. I stroke my mustache and, in my solitude, I wait. *God does not ask a person more than he can give.* The doorbell rings. I open the door and in walks Umm Ali in a gray coat and a white veil wrapped around her plump, tanned face.

"How are you, sir?"

"Fine, Umm Ali, praised be the Lord."

"Winter doesn't seem to want to spare us."

Typical of one for whom time is money, she takes off her coat, hangs it on the hanger near the door, and marches into Fawwaz and Hanaa's bedroom. I follow her as I have been told to do. I sit on a chair and watch her as she sweeps, dusts, cleans, polishes, and puts things in order. Energetic and light in spite of her corpulence. They're afraid she might steal something. Unjustified suspicions, a vestige of the past. Umm Ali's hour is worth one pound. She buzzes around from house to house like a bee. Her income exceeds our combined salaries. But I enjoy being alone with her: a weekly diversion which brings back reminiscences of a bygone dream. Being alone with her disrupts the daily routine.

Thus, divided by the time factor, the old "I" comes face-to-face with the present "I" as they attempt—but fail—to communicate in two very different languages. Then, from its old reserves, the heart steals a fleeting heartbeat whose lifespan lasts but thirty seconds. When she bends forward to unroll the carpet, I imagine that I have gently pinched her. Just a figment of my imagination, for I am completely in control of myself, and she has no qualms whatsoever about me. In fact, she is very much like a man as far as energy, strength, and tenacity go. *O God, forgive us should we forget or err.*

Enjoying the fact that I am alone with her, I ask, "How is the Master?"

"God help him!"

"And the children?"

"They've all emigrated; only the idiot remains. What's the latest with your landlord?" she asks with a laugh.

"He gave up and is now keeping quiet."

"Who would've thought land would one day go mad the way human beings do!"

"Madness is the origin of all things, Umm Ali."

How I love to be alone with you. God forbid! It reminds me of the days of tree-lined Khayrat Street, under the spell of liberal, imported ideas: the mischief of hooligans, and then Fikriya and Ratiba, the two nurses. Life is made up of seasons, and to each its special flavor. Bless those who have loved life for what it is: God's world.

"I envy you for being so fit, Muhtashimi," Sulayman Mubarak, Randa's father, told me one day when I was visiting him.

"Heredity and faith, my dear Mr. Sulayman," I retorted confidently.

Looking in my direction, he inquired slyly:

"Am I to understand that the likes of you believes in fairy tales?"

"God guides whomsoever He wishes."

"Does that imply that, at some point in the past, you were not an atheist?"

"Inherited faith, doubt, atheism, rationalism, skepticism, then faith!"

"An open buffet?" he inquired ironically.

"Rather a life that is complete."

I am proud of being the steadfast sort, happy with next to nothing, and a worshiper of truth. I have implored Zeinab that, when the time comes, there should be no obituary, no funeral, no funeral services, and no mourning.

"The point is that you have grown old and death is now in sight."

A sterile dialogue. *Say, truth has come and falsity has vanished. The false was bound to vanish.* My friend is living in an empty world whilst I am living in a world peopled by loved ones. God forbid! What a visit, that visit of Umm Ali's. What is to become of poor Elwan? Lost amid a circus of crooks.

I talk to him about the good old days in the hope that he would eventually give up on a buffoon who used to let out ten sterile slogans every time he as much as opened his mouth.

Umm Ali is through with her work. She washes her hands and face, puts on her gray coat, and glances at her wristwatch to calculate her due. I give her the money.

"Keep well, sir," she says as she leaves.

"Good-bye, Umm Ali. Don't forget our next appointment."

Back to loneliness. I walk about in the apartment now that it has become difficult for me to walk in the street. The Quran and songs. Bless you who have invented the radio and television. Okra and macaroni for lunch. God has enabled me to derive joy from the act of worship. He has also made me fond of food.

What solitude am I talking about with the world around me packed with millions of people? I love life but will also welcome death when the time comes. So many of my ex-pupils have now become ministers! No monasticism in Islam. Life's but a walking shadow on a summer's day, seeking shelter under the shade of a tree for an hour or so and then is heard no more. I often tell my beloved grandson stories about the past in the hope that he will, for a moment, set aside his woes. I try to encourage him to read but he reads very little. He listens to me in amazement as one who would want to believe what he hears. Forget about Alyaa Samih and Mahmoud al-Mahruqi! Haven't circumstances dampened your faith in your country and in democracy? And why this incomprehensible attachment to a hero long since dead and vanquished?

"So that the world appears not empty, Grandpa." I have drawn your attention to things of utmost beauty.

"All I want now is an apartment and a decent dowry," he says with a laugh.

How can I forget the woes of the world when I think of my beloved grandson? The miracles of holy men are verily a wondrous thing!

Elwan Fawwaz Muhtashimi

Our times have taught me to think. They have also taught me to be contemptuous of everything and suspicious of everything. Should I happen to read about a project which buoys one's spirits and gives one hope, then, all too soon, the truth is revealed and it turns out to be just another dirty trick. Should one let the ship sink? It's just a Mafia which controls us, no more, no less! Where are the good old days? There were, no doubt, some good days. I, too, have known them, the days when my sisters were living in our apartment and it was full of life and warmth. And there were no heavy burdens then. We could also feel the presence of my father and mother at home.

In those days, there was a dialogue of sorts and laughter, the excitement of studies and the illusion of heroism. We are the people. We chose you from the very heart of the people. Love was a bouquet of roses wrapped up in hope. We lost our very first leader, our very first prima donna. Another leader—one diametrically opposed—then comes along to extricate us from our defeat and, in so doing, ruins for us the joy of victory. One victory for two defeats. We chose you from the very heart of the people.

My sweetheart pulls the hook out of the water; it is empty but the hook pierces my thumb which leaves an indelible mark, one that has remained to this very day. On the banks of the River Nile in front of our home, I told her that she was no good at fishing but that she had hooked me all the same, and I have bled. A slow and gradual change took place as friendship turned to love just like the sudden budding of the leaves on a tree at the beginning of spring, something you can only see if you look very carefully. Femininity, cheeks abloom, and the embroidery on the bodice of her dress: a language in which words say one thing and imply another.

Innocence gave way to negotiations and supplications for just a peck on the cheek or lips. The sweetest fruit on the tree: manners, brains, and beauty. It annoys me sometimes that she will appear the more rational of the two. I will never forget the look in her eyes when I confessed that I could not possibly opt for the "sciences" at school: a long dialogue which never actually materialized but one which has always remained there, lurking in some corner. Our families have both fallen in the abyss of the *Infitah*. What grieves me most would be to see you unable to wear the type of clothes that match your beauty. What responsibilities lie ahead!

"Let's amuse ourselves by counting our enemies," I once told her at the Pyramids Resthouse.

"The *Infitah* monster and those expert crooks," she said, joining in the game.

"Would killing a million people be good enough?"

"Killing just one person would be good enough!" she said, laughing.

"Today you're Randa al-Mahruqi," I said, laughing too.

My boss, Anwar Allam, summons me to his room and asks me to visit him at home at five o'clock in the afternoon so as to undertake a comprehensive revision before drawing up the end-of-year accounts. I told Randa about it. She made no comments.

His flat is in a fairly new building in Dokki facing one of the entrances to the October 6th Bridge. He greeted me cheerfully, clad in suit and all.

"Don't be taken aback by the grandeur of the flat. You see, my sister lives with me and she's a rich widow," he said, as though he were trying to dispel any potential suspicions.

Everyone today is suspect. We worked assiduously until eight o'clock. Meanwhile, the widow walked in to serve tea. He introduced us, presenting her as "my sister Gulstan." From the very first glance, I felt I was in the presence of a woman who was forty to fifty years old, not bad looking, a little on the plump side but pleasantly so, and quite attractive in spite—or rather because—of her poise and sense of decorum. She did not sit down but just said, as she was getting ready to leave:

"Ask your guest to stay for dinner with us."

"That's an order!" said Anwar Allam.

Dinner consisted of grilled meat, diverse salads,

cheese, and olives, followed by custard pudding and apples. As we were having dinner, I could hear Anwar Allam saying:

"I handle her affairs, for she has inherited from her husband two buildings and investment certificates."

I was struck by the fact that he wanted to let me know what she actually owned. I imagined more than one reason for his doing so. Then—on a compassionate note— he went on to tell her all about the problems involved in my engagement.

"This is how it is for an entire generation."

"What makes matters worse is that Elwan is a man of principles!" said the man.

"It's wonderful to hear that. To have principles is the most important thing in the world," she said with admiration.

Her tone is indubitably sincere. I find her most attractive. I turn into gunpowder when I'm excited. I really do have problems this way.

"My sister is perfect from all points of view except for one thing on which we disagree, and that is, her turning down more than one good offer of marriage," said Anwar.

"I'm not to be bought and sold. Besides, those are not men," she said calmly.

"A woman's fortune is a legitimate asset, and this shouldn't be taken against the man as long as he gives her her due, and then there are all the other advantages," remarked Anwar Allam.

"No man is to be trusted nowadays," said Madame Gulstan.

"Excuse me, sir, but why are you still not married?" I asked my boss in an attempt to change the subject.

"For many reasons," he answered somewhat vaguely.

"He's wrong, for he could easily get married," added Gulstan, noticing that he hadn't mentioned a single reason.

He then went on to ask me about my family and Randa's. My answers were frank but curt.

"Randa is a wonderful girl but time is getting the better of her," he said.

A stab, and what a stab! Was it deliberate or accidental? Anyway, it ruined the evening for me. Neither did things get any better when Gulstan said:

"One's real age is measured in terms of love."

I left the house, furious at the man and roused by his sister.

Randa Sulayman Mubarak

Anwar Allam signed the letters I had translated and I was on the point of leaving when he leaned back on his swivel chair and said:

"Miss Randa, I have a story that will interest you."

I wonder what it is?

"She was a young doctor engaged for many years to a colleague of hers, also a doctor. They despaired of ever getting married and broke off their engagement. She then married a rich merchant from Wikalat al-Balah and consented to stay at home as a simple housewife," he said.

"Why do you think this story would interest me?" I asked him calmly, although I was both astounded and indignant.

"What do you think of this woman doctor?" he asked me, ignoring my question.

"I can't judge someone about whose circumstances I know nothing," I answered somewhat dryly.

"I consider her smart: better a housewife than a doctor who's a spinster!"

I took leave of him with a look of utter indignation. He eyed me covetously in a way that simply cannot be ignored. In fact, he's a burden on us both—Elwan and me.

On Friday morning, we went to the Pyramids Resthouse. That was after his visit to Anwar Allam. It's truly cold but the sun is out, and here we are looking from up above onto the city, which looks great, calm, and vast, as though free from worries and dirt.

"How was your visit to the Right Honorable Director?" I asked as we were having our tea.

He told me all about it in some detail and succeeded in ruining that lovely morning for me.

"It doesn't seem to have been much of a business call," I said.

"But we did work for three consecutive hours."

"You know what I mean," I said defiantly.

"He's a nerve-wracking person," he said angrily.

"And his sister?"

"Poised and reasonable. I respect her as one would one's own mother."

"And did she treat you as a son?" I asked, laughing coldly.

"Randa, am I being accused and tried?" he inquired on a note of protest.

"God forbid!" I retorted quickly.

I then told him what had gone on between us in his

office. He frowned and cried out, "I shall ask him not to interfere in what doesn't concern him."

"It would be wiser to simply ignore him so that the relationship between you both does not deteriorate," I pleaded.

"The problem is that my position vis-à-vis you is weak, and I don't know how to defend it," he said resentfully.

"You're not being accused and I'm not asking you to put up a defense," I said gently.

"I'm responsible for this and I feel unhappy."

"There's nothing we can do about it."

"But he's a miserable wretch, and is clearly up to something."

"Disregard him and his cheap, vile ways."

We grew silent for a while, seeking refuge in nature until I could hear his plaintive voice saying:

"It's as though we've forgotten all about love."

"We don't need more of it," I said, concealing my own unhappiness.

"I love you," he said, casting a look of desire in my direction.

"I love you," I said, touched to the core.

"I wonder what grand adventure is in store for us now that we're in need of money?" he remarked, perplexed.

"Maybe you'll discover you have the talent of a young premier on the screen?" I said, smiling.

"How about you? Have you tested your voice, even if only under the shower?" We laughed in spite of our worries.

"The problem isn't just one of salary; it's a problem of both key money and furniture," he said.

"Al-Mahruqi simply got married, but he's living in a camp with his sect," he continued after a period of silence.

I imagined the camp and his life as though it were fiction, not fact. In spite of this, my heart went out to him. A simple tent but one suffused with love. I was overwhelmed by a certain feeling of tenderness.

"I want you more than anything else in this world," he said, echoing my own yearnings and desires.

I have always had self-control, ever since I was very young. I have always triumphed over my indomitable desires. The experiences I have witnessed at close quarters have not marked me. I have conservative views on freedom, and I have not been ruffled by the usual sarcastic jibes at my expense: reactionary, unprogressive. Neither have I been spared unhappiness.

Muhtashimi Zayed

Last night, I beheld, as in a dream, our master Abu Dharr. Worship endows me with a certain clarity of vision. But because I love the world, I cannot cross over to the other side. I am suddenly reminded of the following story: Muhammad Ibn al-Attar said: "Sheikh Muhammad Rahin one day asked me: 'What is your heart like?' When I mentioned this to our master Shah Naqshaband, who was standing there, he suddenly stepped on my foot and I fainted. In my state of unconsciousness, I was made to see all of existence concentrated in my heart. When I came to, he said: 'If the heart is thus, how could it possibly be fathomed?' That is why we are told in the Hadith: *'Neither can my earth or sky contain me. But the heart of my faithful worshiper can.'*"

When I recall this story, I cannot help envying the saints and yearning for miracles. But here I stand on the brink of Sufism, clinging on to the joys of worship, content that it is there at the very heart of God's world. My calm, contemplative vision bathes in the light of the Giver. Neither do I regret the stages of life through which I have passed, for each stage has bestowed upon me its own particular light. Do unto the world as though you were to live forever, and unto the hereafter as though you were to die tomorrow.

Around noontime, the doorbell rings. Who is it? Today isn't Umm Ali's day. I open the door and in walks Zeinab Hanem, Randa's mother. I welcome her warmly. I am amazed at her corpulence given her meager means. She seats herself in the living room as I turn off the radio.

"I have no one but you, Muhtashimi Bey," she says. I wonder what on earth has got hold of her.

"We are all in God's hands," I said.

"I should have been speaking to Fawwaz Bey and Hanaa Hanem, but they're so busy working that they've no free time. And it's no use addressing Elwan either. That's why I'm resorting to your good offices."

Now I understand everything even before she as much as utters a single word. She has come to discuss Elwan and Randa's problem.

"I'm at your service, Zeinab Hanem."

"You judge, Muhtashimi Bey. The girl is on the verge of utter ruin."

"God forbid!"

"As far as we're concerned, you people are our first choice, but for how long is she supposed to wait?"

I could sense danger encircling my dear grandson.

"Zeinab Hanem, isn't Randa old enough and sufficiently educated to be able to distinguish between what is good and what is bad for her?"

"Love misleads, Muhtashimi Bey. And, nowadays, love has become a god. Was yours a love match, Muhtashimi Bey? Was Fawwaz Bey's a love match?"

"But they believe in it."

"Are we to let it ruin them both?"

I let out an audible sigh as one clearly helpless. With her double chin swinging up and down, she added:

"Let us then do what we can to save them, and may God help us. Maybe each of them will eventually find the person who suits him best."

"Is Sulayman Bey of your opinion?"

"He's her father just as I'm her mother. But we're both sorry for Elwan. He's a good boy and deserves the very best."

"He's also very unlucky," I muttered as the discussion was coming to a close.

On her way out, she said:

"God help us! Remember, I'm counting on you."

What a morning! I have been forced to act as the harbinger of ill news to the one person dearest to my heart. I sank back in my seat in a state of profound gloom.

At lunchtime, I did not refer to the visit but waited until I could be alone with the young man in the living room. He had naturally not fathomed the meaning of my furtive glances.

"Will you forgive my talking to you about something unpleasant?" I finally asked.

He threw an apprehensive glance in my direction and sarcastically said:

"This is basically the way all stories go, Grandpa."

"About Randa, Elwan."

His handsome face was suddenly transformed as it lit up with feelings of love. I told him what had happened in detail. He clenched his fist and brought it close to his lips as he rested his elbow on an old table.

"It is as though I were a criminal wanted for murder, Grandpa," he said.

"We should think calmly and courageously."

"I'd like to have your impressions, Grandpa."

"We've got to admit that they've got a point," I said, becoming increasingly edgy.

"Randa's not under age," he said sharply.

"No, but that waiting seems endless."

"I'm not to blame."

"Nobody's blaming you."

"Is the final word theirs or hers?"

"Now it's in your hands."

"In mine?"

"Time is flying. You're a reasonable young man and you can save her. You could even save yourself. It's not only bad luck. It's a long line of calamities: June 1967, the *Infitah*, Russia, the United States, and the kingdom of the corrupt."

"And what if I insist on rejecting the idea?" he asked.

"Do what you think is right," I replied.

"I promise to do just that, Grandpa," he said somewhat vaguely, shaking his head.

Fawwaz and Hanaa were told about it that evening.

Hanaa flew into a temper and said she had never felt comfortable about that engagement and had unwillingly consented to it. As for Fawwaz, he said he had always warned his son that this would be the inevitable outcome.

"The engagement is an obstacle to both of them," he said.

"Try to convince him, Uncle. He always resists us but gives in to you. If he had listened to me from the very start, we wouldn't have reached this humiliating point," said Hanaa, addressing me.

I was suddenly reminded of the glorious Sura: *The foolish ones will say they were not turned around from the goal they had set for themselves. Say: To God is the East and the West. He guides whomsoever He wishes on to the right path.*

Elwan Fawwaz Muhtashimi

Winter has come to an end. It is an amazingly clear day. What evil exists lies buried within me alone. I should have chosen some place other than the Pyramids Rest-house. This place situated on the edge of the plateau holds for us the fondest of memories. That calm look in her eyes makes me feel even guiltier. No one deserves respect; nothing is truly worthwhile; no promise is worth keeping. History is on the decline, what with the dark nightingale on the one hand and the dark crow on the other. Dr. Alyaa should cease spouting slogans for she's a wife and a mother. She herself has drained the cup of love to the dregs, so kindly allow us now to sip our cup of tea in peace. Rather, you enjoy it, for I myself am unable to relish it.

"For heaven's sake, why this silence?"

I gazed at the tops of the palm trees scattered along the slope.

"Randa, did you know of your mother's visit to my grandfather?" I asked.

"It didn't go too well but then there's nothing new under the sun," she said scornfully.

"If this were so, we would've got married years ago," I retorted in distress.

"I notice you're more upset than I'd imagined."

"I've been suffocating."

"But we're used to resisting opposition."

"For how much longer?"

"Time isn't important."

"Whether we like it or not, time is important. I've also heavy responsibilities."

"I too have responsibilities. We're in exactly the same position," she said firmly.

"I've got to admit I'm ruining your future."

"And what about your future?"

"It's different. A man can get married in his fifties."

"For the first time, I sense that you feel defeated, Elwan," she muttered, her face growing pale.

"Maybe it's because I've been able to overcome my selfishness for the first time," I said after some hesitation.

"My God, are you seriously considering . . ." she cried, bewildered. She had hardly finished her sentence when I interrupted:

"I now free you from my bondage," I said digging into my own wound.

"Elwan, I can't stand hearing you say that," she said with great emotion.

"Reconsider our position away from my insufferable presence."

"I'm free and no one has any power over me."

"The matter has to be reconsidered."

"It's sound logic but I doubt its soundness where true love is concerned," she said gloomily.

"Careful, don't start doubting me and don't make matters worse, for love, too, has been sacrificed," I said hastily and emotionally.

"You don't have to make any sacrifice."

"I'm only doing what I think is right."

"Just say that you now feel I'm an obstacle in your way," she said bitterly.

"God forgive you, Randa. I shan't sit and defend myself."

"I won't have you make any sacrifice."

"But I insist on it," I said quite plainly.

We were divided by silence, a silence heavier than the approaching night. We both shrank within our shells. Despair was driving us far apart so that our being together seemed to have lost all meaning.

"There's no point in my remaining here," she grumped, standing up.

So I too rose, lifeless. We looked like two strangers, each heading for his own country. Only pain is stronger than love. I could just visualize the loneliness lurking there at the end of the road. We did not exchange a single word all the way back. And no farewells as we parted inside the old building.

My parents were in their room and my grandfather was sitting all alone in front of the television. I sat next to him; he glanced my way furtively and expectantly.

"A film about a mad woman. I don't like it," he said

finally, as though he were trying to escape from his own thoughts.

"Why do you sit and watch something you don't like?" I asked.

"There's a speech on the other channel."

"Why don't you switch it off then?"

"It's better than nothing."

"We broke off our engagement!" I said.

A look of gloom and frustration crept into his eyes.

"God help you in your predicament," he muttered.

"We broke up and that's it," I said dryly.

"I feel guilty," he added in a sad tone.

"You're not responsible, Grandpa," I answered coldly.

Randa Sulayman Mubarak

I could see the image of my face reflected in the look with which my mother greeted me: pity and something very close to fear.

"Congratulations. Your efforts have succeeded," I told her within earshot of my father. She sank into a deeper silence as tears began to fill her eyes. Suddenly my father said:

"I trust the soundness of your judgment."

"Papa, please don't treat me like a child," I said on a note of protest.

"You won't regret it, and I'll be soon reminding you of this," he said calmly.

My mother finally spoke out and said:

"You're a true believer and one therefore doesn't have to worry about you."

"Your mother wasn't wrong, Randa," said my father. This is, however, a brand-new life I shall have to be facing from now on, a life in which there is no trace of Elwan, one which I will have to patiently endure until I die. I was suddenly struck by the bitter sense that I was growing old, haunted by bleak visions of spinsterhood. My bedroom seemed old and shabby with its two ancient beds, its peeling cupboard and faded carpet with only traces of a design still visible. Even my sister Sanaa had become exasperating and nasty.

"You deserve to be congratulated," she said coldly.

I was angry with Elwan. He proved to be weaker than I had imagined. He deserves to remain confused and aimless forever and ever. I can even see him getting into bad ways or selling himself to a woman like Gulstan. The fact is he's tired of having to bear responsibilities. He's trying to escape from this sense of inadequacy and imagines that no one will ever accuse him any longer of not being able to get married. I told myself that I should be congratulating myself on my freedom. I am lighter than I have ever been in the past. He has abandoned me; he has betrayed me. Who but him is ever to care about my excruciating unhappiness? I should be congratulating myself on my freedom. From now on, I can weigh matters rationally with a mind unfettered by the whims of the heart. I am free. . . . I am free! Enough of that! But what did Anwar Allam mean when he spoke to me? What endless unhappiness is that! Does time really cure one from the pangs of love? When and how, damn it! The more I am humiliated, the more contempt I have for him. My parents are being deliberately elusive and will probably remain so until they are once again able to handle matters. First comes defeat in victory, then the sense of victory. He fled and I have been freed. Nurse your pain courageously until it disappears.

I braced myself to meet him on his arrival at the office in the morning, bent on greeting him like any other colleague as though nothing had happened, determined to appear indifferent. But I could not. I was unable to look his way, thus revealing my unhappiness. I wonder how he spent the night? Had he shared my torment or did he sink deep in sleep, a restful sleep, the sleep of freedom? Our secret was going to have to be disclosed. It became known at the office and, on the face of it at least, a sense of gloom seemed to prevail. No one made any comment. The bankrupt must have rejoiced, for unhappy people find solace in like company.

When my turn came to appear before Anwar Allam, he seemed unusually serious at first. However, before I was allowed to go, he said:

"I've been told and am sorry!"

I kept quiet.

"But this was the inevitable end. I even believe it has come rather late in the day," he continued. "A person like you should not have her future depend on a vague promise as though you had no idea of your real worth," he added in a stronger tone.

I did not utter a single word, so he went on:

"When I once said that every problem had a solution, I had this end in mind. And, seeing that everything eventually disappears, sorrow will certainly not be the exception to the rule!"

Returning to his files, he added:

"My advice to you, Miss Randa, is that you should

always remember that we are living in the age of reason. You should trust it blindly, for anything that goes counter to reason is false, false, false!"

Throughout our conversation he was eyeing me boldly. The barriers erected earlier were no longer there. I did not feel that he was more repulsive than before or less so; it was just that I no longer considered it a strange thing.

"I'd like to clarify something, Randa. If he were really and truly sincere, he wouldn't have ever given you up," said my father that evening.

Father is sarcastic and suspicious of people. He digs behind every good deed until he finds a nasty interpretation for it.

"He had to make a painful sacrifice because he could no longer bear to be blamed. I know him better than you, Papa," I said, although I was half inclined to believe him.

"I predict that yours will be a happy end," he said, smiling. When I failed to comment, he added, "Since we have freed ourselves from love, let us place our faith in reason. And then, there's no escaping people's opinion."

"It's a matter that concerns me alone," I retorted, annoyed.

"No. It concerns us all."

Too bad; Elwan recedes far, far away and here we are talking about a new life.

Muhtashimi Zayed

Praise be to God! All is fine were it not for Elwan's sorrow. This year spring is pleasant: the *khamasin* winds are rare. But when will Elwan cheer up and get over it? Praised be the Lord! The day goes by in worship, the recitation of the Quran, food, songs, and films. When one is eighty, one can expect the arrival of the inevitable guest at any time. O God, may it all end well! O God, spare us the anguish and pain of old age, and sprinkle the dewdrops of Thy mercy upon this old house!

God's world is beautiful, worthy of all one's love. What is this evil spell that has been cast upon it? The sky, the River Nile, the trees, the pigeons, and this wondrous voice:

Surely in the creation of the heavens and the earth and the alternation of night and day and the ship that runs in the sea with profit to men, and the water God sends down from heaven therewith reviving the earth after it is dead and His scattering abroad in all manner of crawling things, and the turning about of the winds and the clouds compelled between heaven and earth—surely these are signs for a people having understanding.

If only I could be left to myself in my old age, I would be truly happy. But I am not left in peace. Cheers, then, to the days of naive faith as they filter through the memory, to the days of skepticism fraught with conflict! Here's to the days of heresy involving bold and daring challenges and the days of reason with their interminable discussions! And, finally, cheers to the days of faith and hope! Death is now the last of the promised adventures. Its imminence helps alleviate one's burdens. It will reveal itself at some point and I shall gently say: Pluck the fruit now that it is at its ripest.

One day as I was talking to Elwan about the new television series, he remarked:

"Grandpa, I congratulate you on your peace of mind."

His words disturbed me.

"There is protest in your voice, Elwan," I replied.

He laughed politely but said nothing, so I continued:

"There's a last stage called old age. I stretch out my hand to grip the ring of the eighties at the peak of the mountain. I am now entitled to brood on my last days, leaving the woes of my country to its sons. In my days, I fulfilled my obligations to the best of my abilities. I tried my best to inculcate in you a sense of commitment. But I shall continue to warn you of the perils involved in premature aging. Your glossary consists of only one hero: a martyr. You spend days totally infatuated and spellbound; you are now wasting more time feeling confused and sorry for yourself. The least I can say about myself is that I have lived to see three of my pupils become ministers!"

"Do you consider this one of your achievements, Grandpa?" he asked, laughing.

I could not help laughing out loud myself.

"It may not be, but let history judge. You are faced with challenges fit to create heroes, not a lost generation!" I said. I patted his arm affectionately and went on, "Do your duty as opportunity arises so that you may ultimately be able to devote yourself to God with a clear conscience."

Had only God endowed me with the power of working miracles, I would have found him a flat and made provisions for a dowry, but man proposes and God disposes. All he does now is struggle with his pain and wounds, and I can only pray for him. I recall the cynicism of Sulayman Mubarak, Randa's father, years back.

"Has the wily dervish forgotten the bad old dissolute, happy-go-lucky days?"

"Love has replaced fear between God Almighty and myself," I replied with a smile.

"You compete wholeheartedly with Satan and then aspire to forgiveness."

"Even the dissolute old days I cherish among the fondest of life's memories."

"Hear, hear! Marvel at that modern dervish," cried the man sarcastically.

"You fool! I have reached a point at which I can

detect a Sufi strain in the song: 'I am loved by many a one but it is you who are on my mind.'"

He let out a loud burst of laughter and then inquired:

"And how would you interpret the song: 'The day I was bitten . . .'?"

"Mock to your heart's content. The whims of the venerable teacher discreetly concealed behind a sedate front were but a naive thanksgiving prayer."

"Muhtashimi, I testify that you are the rightful patron of the brothels on the Pyramid Road and the dens of the *Infitah* smugglers," he then cried out.

The real problem is Elwan. I wonder if he considers me responsible for his unhappiness?

"Elwan, I would like to know how you feel about things."

"The fact is I don't quite know what to do with my life," he said, irritated.

"The country will, one day, reach the shore safely."

"I will have become an old man before that happens."

"And he creates what you know not," I sighed.

"Grandpa, you so easily seem to find solutions in beautiful words."

"Elwan, when I was in my thirties, I was fired from my job on the charge of instigating students to go on a strike. I was, at the time, responsible for a family and children and exceedingly poor. I taught at the National Secondary School for a mere pittance. I also held the accounts of a grocer, a friend of mine. We spent a whole year eating nothing but lentils. Ask your father, he can tell you."

He was only half listening to me.

"I have come to hate myself," he then said angrily.

"This may be the sign of a new birth," I said jokingly.

"Or a new death," he replied sarcastically.

"Let our conversation center on life not death!" I cried.

"Death is also life!" he retorted sharply.

And I could hear the echoing of the glorious Sura:

Whosoever is guided is guided only to his own gain, and whosoever goes astray, it is only to his own loss.

Elwan Fawwaz Muhtashimi

My pride wounded and my heart broken, I wander aim-
lessly about like a stray dog. The heat does away with
the pleasures of walking. Café Riche is a refuge from the
pain of loneliness. I sit and order a cup of coffee, and
prick up my ears. This is a temple where offerings are
made to the late hero, who has become a symbol of lost
hope, hope for the poor and the alienated. Here, too,
torrents of indignation are poured upon the hero of victory and peace, victory that has turned out to be but a
dirty game, and peace, surrender. All this within earshot
of Israeli tourists. I find solace in just sitting there listening.

   If this kind of talk disturbs you, then just take a look
at the street. Watch the passersby closely: ceaseless,
uninterrupted, brisk motion. Sullen faces. What do they
conceal? Men, women, children, and even pregnant
women no longer stay at home: the tragic or the comic

sums them all up. Furniture stores and boutiques are all crammed with goods. How many nations live side by side in this one nation? The lights in the square are bright and nerve-wracking, and equally exasperating are the bottles of mineral water on the tables of tourists. And what about us. What do we drink? And then the weirdest songs blast out from crazy radio stations in taxicabs. Only the trees and buildings remain the same. Some speech on the radio is being broadcast from some place. Lies fill the air and mingle with the dust. Fatigue, fatigue . . . Let's return to the gossip: a tiny place falling in ruins selling for a hundred thousand pounds, academic crimes in university circles. How many millionaires are there? Relatives and parasites, smugglers and pimps. Shiites and Sunnis. Stories far better than the *A Thousand and One Nights*. The waiter has a story and so does the shoe-shine boy. When will the famine begin? Open bribes at top voice. The confiscation of lands. And who will cause sectarian rifts to flare up again? The People's Assembly was a place for dancing; it has now become a place for singing. Imports with no transfer of funds. Different kinds of cheese. New banks. What do eggs cost today? The showering of banknotes on singers and dancers in nightclubs on the Pyramid Road simply as a token of appreciation. And the breaking up of the engagement! What did the Imam of the mosque say within earshot of the soldiers of the Central Security Forces? No public lavatory in the entire district. Why don't we rent it furnished? He's nothing but a failed actor. My friend Begin; my friend Kissinger. The uniform is Hitler's; the act, Charlie Chaplin's. Total silence as a woman coming up the street proceeds toward a brothel behind the café. A parallel is drawn between the swelling of her buttocks and public inflation in general. An optimist insists that she works in order to amass the necessary funds for her doctoral dissertation and that her heart is as good as gold. A homosexual proposes homosexuality as a means of solving the crisis of love among the classes with a fixed income and also as a means of achieving the objectives of family planning. A return to the Arabs and war, an everlasting war, and woe unto the agents of normalization. Enough, enough! There's little time for dallying. Trying to escape from you is futile, Randa. Love sickness is cured only slowly and I'm afraid that it might be one of those chronic ill- nesses. The only consolation in my having harmed her is that I have been twice as hard on myself.

Looking at my parents at dinnertime, I quite envied them. Work has relieved them of many worries: work has consumed them. That's a good thing. Not as I had imagined.

"Spare us this talk of yourself and the country! You would imagine we were toiling away just for your sake. Solve your own problems by yourself and let God han- dle those of the country," they told me quite firmly.

I can still recall my father's enthusiasm. He hailed the Revolution, mourned its defeat, and was quite ruined by the *Infitah*.

"The days go by and I find time neither for a haircut nor for paring my fingernails," I have heard him say. "I shove myself into the bus and draw Hanaa close to me to shield her from the eyes of the hungry. On Friday—

our day off—obligations pile up: one must find time for a bath, for condolences, for apologies, and then there's just one hour left for relaxation, during which I'm swamped by your worries and those of the country."

In my state of confusion, I run into my professor at the Graduates' Club. Professor Alyaa, I have broken off my engagement. She thinks it is wrong, and asks me to arrange for a meeting between her and the two of us. Farewell, Professor! Gone are the days of idle talk. I promise you I shall be a staunch enemy of words for the rest of my life. It seems to me that al-Mahruqi has solved his problems by simply defecting. He believes he has had the upper hand, manipulating the times to serve his own ends. What has he done with himself? He has learned the skills of plumbing and has thrown his certificate in the nearest dustbin. I asked him: How about the store?

"I walk about carrying a bag of tools and cry out: Plumber! Plumber! On the spot, I'm showered with requests for repairs. I shall soon be richer than Sayyidna Zubayr," he said, not smiling, for rarely does he smile.

"I invite you to join a new religion called Islam, that is, 'surrender.'"

When I found myself alone in the company of Anwar Allam, he said:

"I'm sorry but I think you did the right thing. Now the world will be a happier place for you."

A few weeks later, he asked me to stop over at his Dokki flat for some urgent work. When the job was done, he invited me to dinner. I had been expecting that from the very start. Nor was I surprised when Gulstan joined us. She intimated in passing that she was sorry about the engagement. Then the conversation centered on modern singing. Anwar Allam made us listen to a variety of tapes.

"You seem to like it, sir."

"To say the least, I don't dislike it," he remarked casually.

Gulstan and I exchanged fleeting glances which revealed unconcealed sympathy: warm, deep, and furtive. She makes no attempt to hide her charm or poise, as though she were telling me: I'm a virtuous woman but I cannot help exuding charm. How about this for feminine wiles besetting young men? As far as I'm concerned, it's first and foremost a matter of hunger. She may consider me a lamb, but I myself eye her more like a wolf. What a relief if she would only consent to become my mistress! But how, when, and where?

"In a month's time, at the very most, Gulstan's new villa will be ready and she'll move in, leaving me here all alone," said Anwar Allam.

To keep the conversation going, I asked:

"Why don't you move in with her, sir?"

"I'm thinking of getting my flat ready for settling down. It's about time I got married!" he replied.

Randa Sulayman Mubarak

Time begets hope: it too brings about both death and life. Some day the microbe will be killed and recovery will be in sight. God will not forsake a true believer. Now we actually talk to each other and collaborate as would two colleagues working in the same office, like colleagues, indeed, but also like strangers who have never tasted the sweetness of a kiss. And sometimes, like me, he invites pity. I no longer condemn him but neither do I respect him. I am now involved in a new experience: Anwar Allam. He is unusually friendly, addressing me in a flirtatious fashion that spells out admiration and sympathy. I have expectations. I sit and brood. My pride will not give in to defeat. Mother now considers the truce to be over and thinks that it is time she spoke up.

"I heard that Ibrahim Bey is ready to propose again," she said one day as we were sitting together in the living room. He's an elderly man, the owner of a mining factory, who had proposed two years ago and was turned down. She seems to have noticed that I was annoyed.

"We've agreed that as long as you have no one in mind, the matter should be settled rationally," she said.

"But he's a widower and a father!" I said, objecting.

"He's also rich, and is ready to accept you just as you are," she pleaded.

"It's not just a matter of buying and selling."

"But we won't find the likes of him easily."

"I'm in no hurry," I retorted sharply.

"Time is running out . . ." she said in a compassion-ate tone.

"I won't be the first spinster in history," I said defi-antly.

My father had kept quiet the whole time. I hadn't been absolutely honest in expressing how I actually felt. The fact is I want to assert myself but not at the expense of my dignity. There should be both money and respect-ability. Anwar Allam has both. Had he been a dubious person, it would have probably been known already. At least, he's acceptable and not physically repulsive. The age difference between us is not unreasonable. As for love, it would be foolish to think about it right now.

I did not have to wait long, for, one morning, after he had ratified the report I held in my hand, he said:

"I would now like to have your opinion."

"What about, sir?" I asked, my heart pounding in anticipation.

"I'm asking your hand in marriage. How about that?" I was speechless, like one struck totally dumb.

"I may not know how to talk about love, but it is

there. I may not be faultless but, I daresay, as far as you're concerned you more than meet all my requirements," he said.

"It comes as a surprise to me," I whispered.

"Of course, you'll need some time to think about it. Fair enough! But allow me to give myself proper credit, for people like me do not embark on marriage unless they are perfectly sure that they are able to shoulder the responsibility."

"Thanks. I'll think about it."

I discussed the matter with my parents that evening.

"That's just fine," said my mother without any hesitation.

"We'll go along with whatever you say," said my father.

When I was alone with my mother, I asked her what she thought we could afford to contribute on our side.

"Nothing on your father's side. As for me, I still have some jewelry which I can sell to get your trousseau ready. The man had better know everything though," she said bitterly.

The bitterness of the experience I had undergone had just about destroyed the hollow masques of diffidence. I had matured in the process far more than I had ever imagined. I insisted on revealing the whole truth, although I had not needed to, for he was already aware of my problem.

"I shall handle the furnishing of the flat and all that," he said quite bluntly.

Naturally I consented.

"We ought to know that the time factor is important

and that everything ought therefore to be settled as soon as possible," he said.

The engagement took place in our flat. The party was restricted to my parents and sisters and, on his side, Gulstan and an elderly brother of his. None of our lifelong friends and neighbors attended. Gulstan offered me a gold necklace encrusted with an expensive diamond.

Deep down, I was tense and nervous, but I did my utmost to control my feelings. I acted my part amazingly well. But when I was alone with Sanaa in our room, I could no longer keep up the show and burst out crying.

"Let this be your last farewell to the sterile past," she said, gazing at me somberly.

"I lost the most precious thing in my life," I groaned in great distress.

"I don't agree with you, but let time take care of everything," she said in an unusual gesture of sympathy.

Muhtashimi Zayed

Above us, just a few steps away, they are throwing an engagement party for Randa. Elwan has just finished getting dressed in a short-sleeved shirt and gray trousers. His forearms are sturdy and the open neckline of his shirt reveals some pitch-black fuzz. His face is sorrow-stricken—youth, beauty, grief. What is brewing deep down within him at this accursed hour? Bitterness, the like of which I have experienced only in poetry. Is there anything I can tell him? I could only conjure up a look and a smile. He greeted me with a wave of his hand.

"Keep well, Grandpa," he said in his usual fashion as he was getting ready to go out.

I suddenly became ill-disposed, like one who has just gulped down a kilo of red and black pepper. I cast aside all thoughts of worship. A mad, miserable world! Dear ones lying underground. So many of you down there. For no apparent reason, memories of you crowd my mind. You have been preceded by hundreds of prophets and saints. The dust is blessed with the best that life has to offer. Why am I being flooded by the past cascading upon me like a waterfall fueled by the power of an active volcano? The cheering of the Revolution echoes anew; total independence or violent death; the people above the King: the fire ablaze in Cairo; the greatness and defeat of him who has passed away; the greatness and setback of his successor. Madness is rampant, breaking its way amid the rocks, bringing in its wake famine and debts. Dear ones who have passed away, so many of you gone. You had not given death a thought. Neither had you reckoned with sickness. And there were those of you who would mix brandy with ginger and chase women on festive occasions. There were others who would tear themselves away from the gambling tables to perform the dawn prayers at the appointed hour. There was even one who threw himself into the waters of the Nile, intoxicated by the light of the moon as the sailboat carrying the big hunks of hashish addicts reeled around him. There were also young men armed with faith and stones who thronged around the policemen and the army challenging them on the anniversary of the annulment of the Constitution. I can still see the battle raging and hear the sound of the bullets and the thumping of heavy, persecuting footsteps. There are so many of you dear ones who have passed away, so many graves oblivious of your fate.

There are also memories of my Azharite grandfather, a teacher of grammar, who used to address my illiterate grandmother in classical Arabic. He begot a progeny of sane and insane offspring who, to this day, perpetrate reason and madness. You scum of the earth, why my grandson? You have bequeathed your children money and security, and the rest of us ruin, poverty, and debts. It is as though the Revolution had taken place only to bring you joy and us sorrow. O God, when wilt Thou give me the courage to spurn the world and what is in it? For how long will I go on yearning for inaccessible miracles? When will I be able to point to the oppressor and slap him down, relieving the world of his evil ways? In fact, the experience has proved to be a failure. We were unable to deal with it for what it actually is: a great blessing. Rather, we soiled it through treachery, egoism, and betrayal.

Here I am walking about in the flat venting my anger, scrutinizing the pieces of worn-out furniture as though I were taking leave of them. At the very center of the headrest of the sofa, I can make out a saying etched out in black Persian script amid a crescent of mother-of-pearl: "Patience is a virtue." O God! What patience are we talking about? We have been waiting for thousands of years until patience has turned to vice and hope to infirmity. I drink a glass of anis and return to my place. A smile suddenly alights on my face. A smile?! Where on earth has it come from? This smile—lost amid great grief—intimates that it has come from far away, from the days when a happy-go-lucky madness broke the barriers of piety. A smile moist with the breath of wine and the sweat of beautiful girls in forbidden spots, from the threshold of my companions of youth, of recklessness and struggle whose peals of laughter blown far away into space have not yet landed on earth. Zumurruda dancing away, almost naked, singing, "I'm knee-high in water." And evenings spent clowning and merrymaking among those outcast for no good reason, evenings where pearls of wisdom would be uttered by whores and madams who would modestly inquire: Are we not more merciful than your great rulers? We are doing our utmost to entertain you whilst they toy with you for their own amusement.

To everlasting paradise, then, Zumurruda, Lahluba, Umm Taqiya, and all of you outcasts to whom we have been ungrateful until a day has come along bringing with it ominous heroes breeding poverty and defeat. Cheers, then, to those nights shrouded in smoke and ecstasy, nights devoted to the art of preening, when no efforts were spared for the sake of others. Content they were with simply eking out a living. And then the rapacity of the others who gloated over the mishaps of the less fortunate. This is what that untimely smile was intimating, a smile alighting on one brokenhearted in a mad world.

There is much regret and an immense yearning for forgiveness. One is ever so weary because there are so many questions about what can or cannot be done, about what should or should not be done whilst the looters are busy sharing the spoils. May God and all miracle workers and learned men step in to put an end to this long night of oppression!

Fawwaz and Hanaa came over to talk to me before retiring to bed.

"What's in store for Elwan?" asked the man.

"All the best. He's strong and will get over his crisis in good time," I said calmly and confidently.

"He's free now and can freely make his own choice," said Hanaa.

"Don't forget that he is the one who made the decision."

I was hoping he would be back before I went in to sleep. An old—but new—idea occurred to me, and that is that one must both love the world and know how to shake off its fetters. Once again, I muttered to myself: so many dear ones gone. Have I really known them that long in this world of ours bent on devouring its own sons?

Elwan Fawwaz Muhtashimi

I played my part unembarrassed. I walked over to where Randa was seated at the office with my hand outstretched. "Heartiest congratulations," I said.

"Thanks and good luck to you," she muttered, throwing a quick glance in my direction. The moment no one was around, I seized the opportunity of telling her a few words from where I was seated close to her.

"I must admit I was hoping you'd make a better choice."

"What's wrong with this one?" she inquired calmly.

"Actually, I want to tell you that you deserve the very best."

"How nice of you!" she said, smiling vaguely.

I told myself that I must close this chapter once and for all. Let us put up with the pain until it disappears altogether. If I give in to grief, I'll go mad. When I heard that the boss had arrived, I immediately went over to him and said:

"Excuse me, I've come to congratulate you."

"Had you not given up on the matter, I wouldn't have given it a second thought myself," he said in a sympathetic tone.

"You always do the right thing."

"Thanks and good luck. From now on, you must think in terms of your own best interest."

I did not know what to say, so he went on:

"The path ahead is clear and all you have to do is think lucidly."

"An excellent piece of advice, sir," I said as I was getting ready to go.

"I've been asked to invite you . . . that is, my sister has invited us to a small tea party to celebrate her moving into the new villa," he said hurriedly.

Indeed the path is clear.

"I'd be happy to go," I said.

I accepted the invitation, although the idea of selling myself had not occurred to me. I went there around six o'clock on a hot and humid evening. The villa was not far from Anwar Allam's building: small and elegant, with a garden full of pink and purple rose bushes. I sat in a brand-new rose-colored living room, with canvas pictures hanging on the wall. Gulstan sat between us, clad in a white dress that accentuated her attractive silhouette.

"The party's limited to just ourselves, for you have been invited as a member of the family," said Anwar Allam.

"He's the only one of your colleagues whose manners I like," said Gulstan softly. I thanked her.

"Indeed, you're quite right," said Anwar Allam with a laugh.

We had tea and I swallowed a big piece of the cake.

"There's talk about the aftereffects of sectarian strife," he went on saying.

"What does this mean?" inquired Gulstan.

"Where's the government?" I asked in turn.

"These are uncertain times," answered Anwar.

"That poor generation of yours has all my sympathy," said Gulstan with compassion, looking my way.

"And rebuke," I added, irritated.

"Excuse me for a few minutes, I have some urgent phone calls to make," said Anwar, standing up.

When we were alone, she drew close to me and murmured gently:

"People like you deserve the very best."

I was wondering what she meant by that. Politics or my own personal tragedy? But I was suddenly aroused by the proximity of her ripe and attractive body. I stared at it with a look of utter shamelessness. All I wanted at the moment was to have her as my mistress.

"I'd like to be alone with you," I whispered, my throat parched.

"I'd be delighted to be alone with a decent person like you," she said sedately.

The electric current running through me came to a sudden halt. She was saying a great deal in the least possible words. Although she had put an end to my reckless dreams on the one hand, yet she seemed to beckon me on the other.

"I respect myself and appreciate those who respect themselves," she said in an attempt to clarify herself.

"I'm very happy to hear that," I said, concealing my disappointment.

"You're welcome to come here at any time. I know a great deal about you, but you hardly know anything about me."

Randa Sulayman Mubarak

He wants to get married as soon as possible and I can find no excuse for procrastinating. We decided to hold the celebrations in Gulstan Hanem's villa. My father, though, was unable to attend. It was a silent party. The buffet was excellent and it was attended by the company's top executives and a group of businessmen. I wore the inevitable mask of joy. In fact, I had long prayed—and was determined—to succeed. I had a genuine desire to try to make it work and to adjust to my new life. What I dreaded most was the possibility of finding Elwan among the guests, but he was not there. Although I was not attracted to him, I did not find him altogether repulsive. Imagine if Elwan had been the bridegroom tonight. What would he have done? I lived my whole life imagining I could not give myself to anyone but him. But, there it is, reality dictates a different set of options. Suffice it that I now feel that I could come to love Anwar one of these days.

In the days that followed, there was an uninterrupted stream of well-wishers, particularly on my side of the family. But what about these men? They come bearing gifts. We welcome them and offer them drinks. Night after night, this wretched stream of men, and some of them are most persistent. I was worn out by these permanent fixtures and by having to exert painstaking efforts at being courteous.

"You've so many friends in the business world!" I told him.

"Actually, they are our future," he replied with a telling bluntness.

"What do you mean?" I inquired, perplexed.

"My job is worthless except in the eyes of a young employee. Our real future is in the private sector, in the intelligent gamble which enables a person to move up from one class to another. So spare no efforts in making them feel at home!"

These, then, are business calls! I did not feel comfortable.

"I had been given to understand that you were financially secure," I said.

"Only in this sense. Other than that there's no sense of security for anyone with this perpetual rise in prices!" he answered blatantly. I was totally dumbfounded while he went on excitedly:

"God won't forgive you if you don't amass an incredible fortune under these circumstances."

"Isn't it enough to have what will allow us to live comfortably?"

"Comfortably? We're in a merciless rat race, my dear."

Here, then, is a new person emerging, with amazing rapidity, from behind that other person. He will not hear of patience nor will he be satisfied with rising gradually. As for my reactions, they're beside the point. He's very simply saying: That's me, pure and simple, with no retouches. How about that? He sees only his own ambitions in this world, and those are his sole concern. He prostrates himself before them in prayer a hundred times a day. It's as though I have no existence apart from the role I may be able to play in his broader strategy. Even those false pretenses of his, he's no good at them, and doesn't even seem to care. He's a total surprise to me, a colossal surprise which strikes me like a thunderbolt. Love is only a thing of the moment. I soon experienced an inconsolable sense of disappointment. I had sold myself for nothing. Or maybe things are even worse than that. I am ashamed to confess my disappointment. I was deluded into thinking that I was, to say the least, an end, and I now discover that I am no more than simply a means to an end, quite worthless other than my function as such. My job here is to be courteous, to entertain, and offer drinks. He was not even satisfied with that, and soon informed me that he could no longer postpone his evening duties and that I would myself have to be responsible for receiving and entertaining guests.

"It's an extension of your public relations job," he said with a laugh.

"But there's nothing in common between those people and myself," I objected.

"It's not important. Suffice it that you are eloquent, intelligent, and cultured. We're partners and are supposed to substitute for one another, particularly when there's ultimately much to gain from it."

"This is the language of the market. I never thought I would have to deal with it!" I said sharply—the first sharp words uttered during our honeymoon.

"The sooner, the better," he said with a smile.

Biting sarcasm. I felt that my experience was rapidly proving to be a failure. I found myself amid men who were drinking, laughing boisterously, leaping to break all boundaries. I could hear a dirty joke now and felt a wave of irritation and anger surging up within me.

"Enough!" I said coldly.

They looked at me gloomily.

"Enough drinking!" I said roughly.

"Were we being impolite?" asked one of them.

"It seems so!" I answered coldly.

"Is this an indication that we should leave?"

"Definitely!" I said, growing angrier.

I was in the sorriest of states as I stood waiting, tormented by misgivings and apprehensions. When he returned around midnight, he turned pale as soon as he set eyes on me, and asked:

"Is everything fine?"

"Absolutely not. This is a house, not a bar."

"What happened?"

"In a word, I threw them out. Interpret it as you wish."

He sank silently into the seat facing me. Following a period of silence, he muttered:

"A great structure has just collapsed."

"On top of a handful of bastards," I shrieked.

"A disappointment."

"Don't you want to understand?" I asked, highly incensed.

"I thought you understood things better," he said in an irritatingly calm tone.

"Actually, I don't understand you. You're a strange person," I continued.

And, again, with his irritating calmness, he added:

"It's simply a misunderstanding."

"A misunderstanding?"

"I mean a misjudgment on my part."

"You are indeed a vile person!" I shrieked.

With a wave of his hand, he indicated that I should control myself and then continued:

"No, no, no need to bring up this subject. I've lived a lifetime without getting angry."

"This speaks for you."

"Calm down. There's been a mistake and it can be corrected."

"I'm going," I said insistently.

"Why the hurry? Wait until morning."

"I shall not remain in this house a minute longer!"

"Do what you please, but no need to get angry," he said, giving up on me.

Muhtashimi Zayed

He loves not the evildoers. What is this decree all about? You declare a revolution on May 5 and then annul it on September 5? You throw all sorts of Egyptians into prison—Muslims, Copts, party men, and intellectuals? Only the opportunists are on the loose. God help you, Egypt!

And whosoever is blind in this world shall be blind in the world to come, and he shall be even further astray from the way.

I remember the day Saad Zaghloul was placed under house arrest in Bayt al-Umma and the opportunists started crawling toward the Palace in a show of affected loyalty. Why are you replaying that old drama that looms large in the repertoire of Egyptian tragedies? I remember the dark days of oppression. Was 1919 then a dream or a myth? (Might does not make right. The mighty are those who can, when incensed, exert self-control.) I wonder what the morrow has in store for us? As for me, I lost my closest and very last friend yesterday. Our friendship lasted seventy-five years, ever since we first set foot in primary school. Were it not for old age and poor means of transport . . . Oh! I insisted on attending the funeral services, a painful journey like the pilgrimage. I leaned on Elwan. Later, during the condolence services, I recalled old memories: school, the street, the café, the pub, student committees, weddings, birthdays. That face and that smile. Have you heard the latest? Complaints about the hardships of life. We saw eye to eye about everything except football: are you for the Zamalek team or the National team? Drink a glass of water on an empty stomach. Don't forget the medicine for the memory. I missed your comments on September 5, but I know exactly what you would have said. The Quranic recitation begins: *Every soul shall taste of death.*

Soon death came along smiling cunningly, and sat beside me. Don't hurry: only one step left. The death of my old friend is a rehearsal for my own death. I can just see the whole thing: the washing of the corpse, its burial, the pallbearers. I read the obituary: Muhtashimi Zayed, sometime educator and supporter of the Nationalist Movement in his youth. Do you remember him? I thought he had died ages ago. Oblivion shuffles by wearily, but I surrender willingly. Indeed, it has been a long life, but now it seems like only a fleeting moment. Love, violence, anger, hope—so many already gone. There is no difference now between your being in the coffin and my walking behind you or vice versa. His son greeted me warmly and told me that, as he was dying, he said: Please remember me to him.

That evening, my son Fawwaz reprimanded me:

"At your age, you can be excused from these types of obligations."

On the other hand, Hanaa was saying:

"Today I bought a priceless book entitled *How to Repair Your Household Appliances*. Let's hope it will liberate us from the plumber and electrician." Whereupon Elwan added:

"Is there no book that can liberate us from the rulers?"

"People are speaking of nothing but the imprisonment of those who have been thrown into jail," continued Fawwaz.

"Professor Alyaa is in prison and so is my friend Mahmud al-Mahruqi!" rejoined Elwan nervously.

"They've promised to hold a quick trial so that whoever is innocent would not be harmed," I added in an attempt to calm them down.

"You still believe those lies, Grandpa?"

Thanks to his state of confusion, he was saved from prison. Woe unto those who are committed!

"I hope you'll muster enough courage to get over your crisis," I told him the moment we were alone.

"When calamities accumulate they lose their sharpness and intensity," he said in an ironic tone.

He switched off the television set and returned to his seat beside me.

"Grandpa, I want to tell you a secret."

I listened to him anxiously as he went on:

"There are strong indications that I'll be approached regarding a potential marriage to the sister of Anwar Allam, Randa's husband."

"Really! Tell me more about it."

"She's a widow, twenty years older than I, and very rich."

"And looks-wise?"

"Not as you expect. She's quite acceptable—and respectable."

When he found that I had kept quiet, he continued:

"What do you say, Grandpa?"

"It's a very personal kind of decision, and it's best you make it alone," I said, trying to overcome my perplexity.

"But I insist on knowing your point of view."

"Do you love her?"

"No, but I don't hate her either."

"I don't know what to say."

"There must be something you can say."

"I have no right to decide her fate. I belong to another world and it would not be wise that my world trespass on another."

"But I'm not used to your being so elusive."

For a while I was silent, and then added:

"There are undeniable advantages to this affair and also undeniable disadvantages. But, in your case, the advantages outweigh the disadvantages!"

"I refuse to sell myself!" he said quickly, with a vague smile.

I immediately felt relieved, but asked him:

"Did you give it enough thought before making up your mind?"

"More thought than necessary."

"God bless you, then, and may He grant you what your heart desires," I said in an emotional tone of voice. "Pray, work your miracles Sayyidi al-Hanafi!" I muttered under my breath.

Elwan Fawwaz Muhtashimi

"Have you heard, Elwan?" said my grandfather as I was getting ready to go out.

As I looked at him inquiringly, he added:

"Randa got a divorce!"

I was seized by a sudden sense of bewilderment, fear, and relief.

"She's still on her honeymoon!" I cried.

"Your mother told me so this morning."

"How could this have happened?"

"When living together becomes impossible."

As he was taking leave of me, I added:

"I wanted to tell you, so it wouldn't come as a surprise to you over there."

As I walked to the office, I was all wrapped up in my own thoughts and emotions, conscious only of my own sorrow and joy. A sense of gloom surrounded Randa, and very soon it had spread all over the office.

"I'm . . ." I said as I greeted her.

"Thanks," she said, interrupting me.

"You don't deserve that," I said with great sincerity.

"Thanks again. And that's enough now," she said calmly.

There were a great many rumors going around in Randa's absence. I heard all sorts of amazing things. It was obvious that he had failed, as often happens with men who get married late in life. No, no, he's queer. . . . Look at the way he gesticulates with his hands. No, but the problem is her frigidity: apparent beauty is not everything. There are also rumors that he's having an affair with his sister. I listened and was hurt. I love you, Randa, as much as I used to, if not more. It hurts me to see you defeated so. My heart goes out to you in your wounded pride.

I thought I might get closer to the truth by resorting to Anwar Allam.

"Thanks!" he muttered sarcastically when I expressed my regret.

"I'm sorry for both of you," I said as soon as I felt that he was doubting my sincerity.

"There's nothing that warrants regret," he said coldly. With not a word more, he returned to the paperwork on his desk.

Gulstan Hanem invited me over. I accepted without hesitation, almost sure that she would tell me the truth. She was all bedecked like a bride.

"You only visit me when I invite you?" she said reprimandingly.

"I don't want to cause you any embarrassment."

"A nonsensical excuse, and you're the first to know that."

She offered me ice cream filled with nuts.

"It just occurred to me," she then said.

I looked at her with interest, and she continued:

"My brother now seems far too busy for me, so how about your handling my affairs?"

The suggestion seemed like a bottomless pit opening up beneath me.

"This may upset him," I said.

"It's his idea!"

"Give me time to think about it, for I have been toying with the idea of enrolling for a master's degree," I said, embarrassed.

"The work is simple but requires someone honest."

"Just give me a little while to think about it."

She suddenly offered to reveal an important aspect of her past.

"My marriage has always made me the object of greed. Actually, it was my father who married me off to a man who was thirty years my senior. In spite of that, I continued to lead an impeccably honest and respectable life. My reputation has remained as good as gold."

"You are the epitome of respect," I said in a tone of despair which passed her unawares. "Anwar Bey is also respectable, yet see how unlucky he is," I added cunningly.

"Are you feeling sorry for him or for his wife?" she asked, looking at me suspiciously.

"What's done cannot be undone!" I said defiantly.

"Really?!"

"That's the truth, plain and simple."

"Then forget about other people's problems and let's concentrate on ours!"

I crouched in a corner, not knowing what to say. Then, with a bluntness that reminded me of her brother, she added:

"You understand and so do I. I've a right to seek my own happiness as long as my dignity remains untouched," she added somewhat excitedly.

Then, in order to break that unbearable silence, I said, "I respect so sound a logic."

"You won't have any regrets. And I'll be waiting," she said sweetly.

Randa Sulayman Mubarak

Six pairs of eyes whirling in a cesspool of confusion: my eyes in my mother's eyes, my eyes in my father's, and my mother's in my father's—all drawing away from each other furtively. My mother was shocked to see me walk in at that time of night. Her face grew pale, reflecting the color of my own face. My father was asleep, covered with a sheet.

"Randa, what happened?" she whispered.

We stood in the center of the hall, and all my pent-up emotions suddenly gushed out at one go:

"I'm getting a divorce!"

I told her the whole story in detail. My father was told about it in bits and pieces after breakfast.

"We can't possibly see things eye to eye," I told him.

My mother then started telling him about the guests and the drinking. His face was flushed with anger.

"Take it easy on your health," I said.

"I now understand everything. If only I had the strength, I would've shown him."

"How come you didn't see through him?"

"Everyone has secrets which he conceals. I shan't deny that I was fooled."

"We'd better consult a lawyer."

"That's the best way to spread the scandal. Actually, he's conceded to all my rights without the least objection," I said.

"This quick divorce may tempt evil tongues to gossip about you."

"I can take that, and pretty soon it will all be forgotten."

Although none of my colleagues said anything, I could sense that the place was fraught with questions, particularly on Elwan's part. I was exceedingly angry with him.

"I'm very unhappy," he whispered one day when we were alone.

"Why?" I inquired coldly.

"Maybe it's a feeling of guilt."

"You've nothing to do with what happened."

"I still love you," he said, averting his eyes from me.

"I don't want to hear this word, please!" I said sharply.

As time went by, everything seemed to aggravate me, even my own anger. I began to feel as sorry for him as I was for myself. I even began to wonder how things were going between him and Gulstan. Would he marry her one day? What's wrong with that? The woman may be better than her brother. There didn't seem to be anything wrong with her. And she obviously wants him. Damn it, she loves him! Who would've thought that one day we would have parted? Who would've thought that our big hopes would have frittered away like a handful of dust? One day, as we were getting ready to leave, he whispered:

"I'm dying to have a few words with you."

My immense desire to talk to him made me as silent as the grave. So we went to the Pyramids Resthouse, where we had some sandwiches with our tea, and kept staring at each other foolishly.

"What are your plans?" he asked.

"I'm living without plans or dreams, which gives me peace of mind," I said quite simply.

"Me too, but Grandpa says that suddenly—"

I interrupted him. "Forget about your grandfather and his quotable quotes. They're of no use to us. When will you marry Gulstan?"

"Who said that?" he inquired, glowering.

"Just a question."

"I don't sell myself."

"You therefore think I sold myself?"

"No, it's a different matter. It's not unusual for a girl to marry a man older than herself, but the opposite . . ." he replied hurriedly.

He scrutinized me carefully.

"Why did your marriage break up?" he then asked.

I had a genuine desire to confess the truth to him, to him in particular, rather than to anyone else.

"Promise not to whisper a word to a single soul?"

"On my word of honor."

So I let out all the feelings bottled up within me.

"The bastard!" he suddenly cried out.

"The time for anger is over. But please don't forget your promise."

"It's beyond one's wildest imagination."

"More amazing things have been heard though."

Muhtashimi Zayed

I dream of my father, my mother, and my sister
Mahasin. I even once beheld them in a parachute floating above my head. Has perchance the time to depart
drawn close? Is it time that the old man spared the country the cost of his pension? I'm in good health in spite of
Sulayman Mubarak's evil eye! Health is ailment enough.
So said the Messenger of God. O Lord! Thy worshipper
is waiting. At any moment he expects to hear the knell
of parting day, and he shall welcome the caller with all
due respect. O Lord, may everything end well! Protect
me from pain and infirmity. I thank Thee for a long and
happy life. Suffice it that I have not harmed a single soul
in the world of ours replete with harm. I have spent my
old days strolling amid Thy words, Thy prophets, and
Thy saints. Earlier I braved the vicissitudes of Thy
world. Worship is now my form of exercise, songs my
entertainment, and lawful food my enjoyment. The feast

comes along adorned with autumnal dewdrops. White clouds gather over the somber River Nile and the towering evergreen trees. These kinds of days are few and far between in the life of this shattered family. Fawwaz relaxes in his *gallabiya,* Hanaa combs her white hair whilst Elwan is busy shaving, getting ready to go out.

"Children, we're finally gathered together as one happy family!" I cried joyfully, looking at them one by one.

"A drop of rest in a sea of fatigue," said Fawwaz in his loud voice.

"Had things been different, we would've gone off to the Qanater Gardens."

"An idea quite out of keeping with the times. Actually, it's a crazy idea."

"We eat and sleep. That's what's left of the feast."

"And you, Elwan?"

"I'll walk over to the Café."

"Gossip as usual!" said Fawwaz with a smile.

"Once again, the feast coincides with another festive occasion—Victory Day," I added.

"Victory and prison," added Elwan ironically.

"Nothing ever remains the same. There's always something new under the sun," I said good-humoredly.

"Really! Long live patience and let's just keep waiting!"

"A new oil dig or the discovery of an unknown river in the desert," mused Fawwaz.

"Or the outbreak of a revolution," said Elwan.

"Does revolution mean more than just added destruction?" surmised Fawwaz.

"To make matters even worse than they are!" cried Elwan sarcastically.

They know nothing of revolutions. They haven't even heard of them. The hired storyteller has told them a false, untrue story. The poor teacher begins his lesson with the treacherous question: What were the causes of the failure of the 1919 revolution?

Goddamn bastards! Have you no drop of decency left? Prison guards ... worshipers of Nero ... There goes Elwan waving to us as he goes by. Off he goes, burdened by his own disappointment and that of his generation.

"Let's watch the celebrations," said Hanaa, switching on the television set.

The general atmosphere is one of immense joy. The President walks by, surrounded by a luminous halo like that of the Night of Fate, clad in his commander's uniform and the king's scepter in his hand. Hordes of dignitaries follow.

"He's ever so pleased with himself," said Hanaa innocently.

"Today's his day," I said.

"He's happy and deserves to be so," said Fawwaz. "He's lost so much since September fifth," he added sorrowfully.

A ground and air parade all at once: a rare sight, not likely to happen again.

"We would see the army only on Mahmal Day," I said in a voice echoing from the past.

"Look, Father, that's a whole other world."

"His face is all pink as though he's smeared it with rouge," said Hanaa with a laugh.

The army units go by and so does time. I start to feel lethargic and sleepy. Then suddenly I wake up at a strange point in time. History and time corner me, saying: That is how the events you skimmed through in history books took place. And now it's happening right here in the living room. The television screen becomes blurred and an unusual commotion follows: voices are heard and then a blackout.

"Fawwaz, is there anything wrong with the television set?"

"Nothing wrong with the set. I don't know what happened."

"Something odd. I don't feel comfortable," said Hanaa in a worried tone.

"Me too," added Fawwaz.

"Is . . . ?" I asked.

"God only knows, Father. Pretty soon we'll know everything."

"God protect us!" I said from the bottom of my heart.

Elwan Fawwaz Muhtashimi

Let this be a festive occasion and let's forget our worries for an hour or so. But how when there are a hundred chinks in the door? What is the River Nile trying to intimate? And the trees? Listen carefully. They're saying, Elwan, you poor fellow, trapped within four walls, Randa is coming back to you in the guise of friendship and small talk, in the guise of undeclared love resting on twin pillars of steel and despair, and shrouded in vague dreams. No persecution from family, no hope, and no despair! March at a brisk military pace, for today is soldiers' day. The café is packed with wordmongers. Here there's no satisfaction and no action. A transistor radio, brought along for the occasion, is placed on one of the tables between us. Just like on the day the late President broadcast his defeat in June 1967. The late President was greater in his defeat than this one in his glory was the first thing I heard. This reminds me of what my grandfather once said: We are a people more given to defeat than to victory. The strain that spells out despair has become deeply ingrained in us because of the countless defeats we have had to endure. We have thus learned to love sad songs, tragedies, and heroes who are martyrs. All our leaders have been martyrs: Mustafa Kamel, martyr to struggle and sickness; Muhammad Farid and Saad Zaghloul, both martyrs to exile; Mustafa al-Nahhas, martyr to persecution; Gamal Abd al-Nasser, martyr to June 5. As for this victorious, smug one, he has broken the rule: his victory constituted a challenge which gave rise to new feelings, emotions for which we were quite unprepared. He exacted a change of tune, one which had long been familiar to us. For this, we cursed him, our hearts full of rancor. And, ultimately, he was to keep for himself the fruits of victory, leaving us his *Infitah,* which only spelled out poverty and corruption. This is the crux of the matter.

We were caught up in the heat of arguments as the loudspeaker and transistor radio broadcast the details of Victory Day celebrations to whoever cared to listen. And, as usual, time got the better of us until, suddenly, strange voices could be heard.

"The traitors . . . the traitors," cried the broadcaster's voice.

Tongues grew paralyzed and eyes were averted as heads crowded around the transistor radio. The broadcasting of the celebrations came to a sudden halt, and then some songs started to be broadcast.

"What happened?"

"Something unusual."

"He said: 'The traitors, the traitors, the traitors!' "

"An invasion!"

"Of whom?"

"Honestly, what a stupid question!"

"The songs being broadcast indicate that . . ."

"Since when has logic meant anything?"

"A little patience!"

We had no desire to go back home. We all just huddled up in an urge to remain all together in the face of the unknown. We had a quick meal of macaroni for lunch and then sat there waiting. Following a brief but violent period of time, the broadcaster announced that there had been an abortive attempt on the President's life, that the President had left, and that the security forces were in full control of the situation. And, once again, there were songs on the radio.

"This, then, is the truth."

"The truth."

"Think a little."

"Certain facts cannot be concealed."

"But they can be delayed."

"Who are the assaulters?"

"Who but those involved in the religious movement?"

"But he was sitting in the very midst of soldiers and guards."

"Listen, they've started to broadcast national hymns."

Suddenly, there was a new broadcast announcing that the President had been slightly injured and that he was getting full medical attention at the hospital. Our hearts leaped up at the thought of increased chances of new possibilities. Time came to a halt, changed its tune, and emerged with a brand-new look on its face.

"The man has been injured. What then?"

"Get ready for prison."

"A definite return to terrorism."

"He'll survive and seek revenge."

"Will we be hearing the Quran after the hymns?"

We whiled away the time that was weighing heavily upon us. Jokes were cracked and then the recitation of the Quran began. At first, we turned pale. It's true then. Amazing! Actually true!? The man's finished? Who would've believed? Why do we sometimes get a feeling that the impossible is actually possible? Why do we imagine that there exists a reality other than death in this world? Death is the true dictator. The official announcement comes to us like a final statement. I wonder what people are saying? I'd like to hear what is being said around us in the café. I pricked up my ears. There is no power or might save in God. To him alone is permanence. The country is in obvious danger. He doesn't deserve this end, whatever his misdeeds. On his day of glory? A plot. Surely there's a conspiracy. No doubt. The hell with him! Death saved him from madness. Anyhow, he had to go. This is what happens to those who imagine that the country is nothing but a dead corpse. No, it's a foreign conspiracy. He doesn't deserve this end. It was the inevitable end. He was a curse on us. He who kills will ultimately be killed. In a split second, an empire has collapsed. The empire of robbers. What is the Mafia thinking about right now? I returned to my seat, torn by conflicting feelings of despair, fear, and joy. Vague hopes hovered overhead, hopes of unknown possibilities, hopes that the prevailing lethargy and routine would, at last, be shattered, and that one could start soaring toward limitless horizons. Tomorrow cannot be worse than today. Even chaos is better than despair, and battling with phantoms is better than fear.

This blow has rocked an empire and shaken fortresses.

By evening, I realized I had started dozing off. All this talk had exhausted me. I felt like taking a walk. There's a trace of death on every passerby. Suddenly, there I am in front of Gulstan's villa. Anwar Allam's car is parked there, awaiting its owner. Sexual desire of every sort takes possession of me and, with it, an irrepressible urge to kill.

Randa Sulayman Mubarak

How awful! Is killing the only way to do it? What do his wife and daughters have to do with it? I'm not for him, but he doesn't deserve this end. It jolts me back to a reconsideration of public problems after having been so long engrossed in my own, private problems. To kill is hideous and God frowns upon it.

My mother sobbed like one untouched by politics. The living room was gloomier than usual at that particular time. I wanted to know what my father thought about all this.

"My opinion will certainly not revive the dead," he said.

He peered at me with faded, tired-looking eyes and went on:

"The country is sick with fanaticism, Randa. Where are the days of 'Why am I a heretic?' They want to drag us fourteen centuries back."

He kept quiet for a while and then added:

"I know you don't entirely agree with me, so suit yourself. However, we do agree on the principle that it is wrong to kill."

This is as much as we can agree on. I wonder where you are, Elwan? You didn't like him. So are you happy that this is how he has ended?

Suddenly, quite unexpectedly after so long an absence, Elwan burst into our flat with a boldness that showed that he was quite disturbed. When we were alone in the dining room, I asked:

"Where were you when it happened?"

"Forget about that! Nothing new there. Randa, listen to me carefully," he said, markedly perturbed.

"What's wrong with you?"

"This evening, I found myself in front of Gulstan's villa. Anwar Allam's car was parked there. Uninvited and quite spontaneously, I burst into the house. He was the first person I saw. He greeted me and said: 'Come in . . . I'm glad you just decided to drop by casually.' I suddenly cried unconsciously: 'You filthy man!' and punched him violently in the chest, whereupon he reeled and fell on the floor. At that point, a scream revealed Gulstan's presence. 'Stop beating him!' she cried firmly. I helped him to get back on his feet and led him to her bedroom. I stood there stock-still, almost unconscious. She disappeared for a quarter of an hour and then returned, her face pale and a bewildered look in her eyes.

" 'You crazy fool, what did you do? You killed him!' she muttered. I just stood there, staring at her.

" 'You crazy fool, what did you do? Why did you kill him?' she mumbled as her eyes filled with tears. Then, exhausted, she collapsed on an armchair and rested her head in her hands as I began to regain consciousness. I was beginning to realize the enormity of my deed.

" 'Call the police. It's my fate,' I finally said.

"She did not move. As for me, I had the strongest urge to disentangle myself from the situation.

" 'I shall go off to the police myself,' I said.

"She made an obscure gesture of the hand and whispered:

" 'Stay put where you are.'

"Time weighed heavily on me, wracking my nerves like a bulldozer.

" 'No point in waiting,' I finally said.

" 'Wait,' she whispered. She bent her head, averting her eyes from me.

" 'He had a chronic heart condition,' she whispered again.

"What is she thinking about? Doubt and then a glimmer of hope.

" 'But it was I who . . .'

" 'There's no trace of blows,' she said calmly, indicating that her troubled mind had begun functioning anew.

"With this statement, she became a partner in the crime. I scrutinized her face in bewilderment, amazed at that aspect of human nature which would, under ordinary circumstances, have forever remained concealed. What a woman! But my joy at the life belt thrown at me was like that of a desperate, drowning man.

" 'Nothing can be concealed from the doctor,' I said.

" 'That's none of your business,' she said with utter confidence.

"We exchanged a conspiratorial look.

" 'Of course, you understand why I'm trying to save you?' she then said.

"I nodded and lowered my head in disbelief.

" 'Can I trust your word of honor?' she then asked.

"I gave her my word of honor."

"Why are you telling me this secret?" I asked when he had finished.

"There are no secrets between us, Randa."

"You committed a crime incensed by what had happened to me. You deserve to be saved," I said bitterly.

"Do you really think so?"

"Of course, I can't possibly condemn you."

"Actually, I haven't told you the whole truth, for after I left the villa, I became thoroughly disgusted with myself, despising the decision I had made. In my state of confusion. I came over to you to confess everything," he said, much moved.

"I understand your feelings very well, but I don't blame you for the decision you've made!" I said compassionately.

"But I won't have it," he said stubbornly, as my heart went out to him.

"That's madness!"

"So let it be."

"Miracles of this sort won't happen again," I pleaded desperately.

"Even so."

"No time for regret."

"I will never regret anything."

"I'm not guilty of what you imagine."

"I shall go back to her to clarify everything," he said.

"I don't think you should."

Muhtashimi Zayed

After Elwan's disappearance, I am reduced to utter lone-liness. As for the world around us, it is aspiring to new hope. How courageous Randa turned out to be: going to court to defend the young man—and with such decency and dignity. It was lucky that the crime was interpreted as beating that resulted in death. Years will go by and then he will leave prison having mastered some skill or other. He will then be in a better position to meet the challenges of life and to realize his hopes. I do not think I shall see him again. But he will find my room vacant and will be able to have it and get married to his sweetheart. Have I perchance lived too long? And have I, unknowingly, played a part in aggravating his problem?

The time has come for me to join the ranks of those who dedicate themselves to the glorification of God in anticipation of eternity in the realm of the All-Exalted.

BOOKS BY NAGUIB MAHFOUZ

ARABIAN NIGHTS AND DAYS
0-385-46901-2

THE BEGINNING AND THE END
0-385-26458-5

CHILDREN OF THE ALLEY
0-385-26473-9

ECHOES OF AN AUTOBIOGRAPHY
0-385-48556-5

THE HARAFISH
0-385-42335-7

MIDAQ ALLEY
0-385-26476-3

WEDDING SONG
0-385-26464-X

The Cairo Trilogy:

PALACE WALK
0-385-26466-6

PALACE OF DESIRE
0-385-26468-2

SUGAR STREET
0-385-26470-4

ANCHOR BOOKS
Visit Anchor on the web at: www.anchorbooks.com
Available at your local bookstore, or call toll-free to order:
1-800-793-2665 (credit cards only).